DRAGON
Gets By

DRAGON'S SECOND TALE

Dav Pilkey

ORCHARD BOOKS · NEW YORK

THE DRAGON TALES

Orchard Books
95 Madison Avenue, New York, NY 10016

Manufactured in the United States of America
Printed by Barton Press, Inc.
Bound by Horowitz/Rae
Series designed by Mina Greenstein
The text of this book is set in 18 point Galliard condensed.
The illustrations are watercolor with pencil, reproduced in full color.
Hardcover   10 9 8 7 6 5 4 3 2
Paperback   10 9 8 7 6 5 4 3 2 1

Library of Congress Cataloging-in-Publication Data
Pilkey, Dav, date.
Dragon gets by / Dav Pilkey.
p.   cm. "A Richard Jackson book."
Summary: Dragon wakes up groggy and does everything wrong all day long.
ISBN 0-531-05935-9 (tr.) ISBN 0-531-08535-X (lib. bdg.) ISBN 0-531-07081-6 (pbk.)
[1. Dragons—Fiction.] I. Title. PZ7.P63123Dr 1991 [E]—dc20
90-46027

Contents

For my old pal, George Hurst

1
Dragon Sees the Day

One warm, sunny morning
Dragon woke up and yawned.
He was very groggy. . . .

And whenever Dragon woke up groggy,
he did *everything* wrong.

First, he read an egg
and fried the morning newspaper.

Then he buttered his tea
and sipped a cup of toast.

Finally, Dragon opened the door
to see the day.
But Dragon did not see the sun.
He did not see the trees or the hills
or the flowers or the sky.
He saw only shadows.

"It must still be nighttime,"
said Dragon.

So he went back to bed.

2
Housework

Dragon's floor was very dirty.
He got his broom and began to sweep.

When he was finished sweeping,
the floor was still dirty.
So Dragon swept again. . . .
And there was still dirt everywhere.

"There sure is a lot of dirt
on this floor," said Dragon.

Dragon swept all morning long,
and into the afternoon.
He carried out wheelbarrows
filled with dirt.

All of his sweeping left
a very big hole in his floor.

Finally, the mailmouse came by.
She looked at all the dirt
outside the house.

She looked at the big hole
inside the house.

"What's going on in here?"
asked the mailmouse.

"I'm sweeping my floor," said Dragon.
"It is very dirty."

"But you have a dirt floor,"
said the mailmouse. "It is made of dirt."

17

Dragon looked at the hole he had swept,
and scratched his big head.

"Looks like you've made a mess,"
said the mailmouse.

"Looks like I've made a basement,"
said Dragon.

3
Yardwork

Dragon looked at the big pile of dirt
in his yard.
"What am I going to do
with all this dirt?" he wondered.

He got a shovel
and dug a big, deep hole.

Then he scooped the dirt into the hole.
"Well, that takes care of that,"
said Dragon.

4
Shopping

Dragon looked in his cupboard,
but there was no food at all.
"The cupboard is bare," said Dragon.
"Time to go shopping."

Dragon got into his car and drove.
The food store was at the top of a hill.
It was a very steep drive.

Dragon loved to go shopping.
He was a very wise shopper.
He bought food only
from the five basic food groups:

He bought cheese curls from the dairy group.
He bought doughnuts from the bread group.

He bought catsup
from the fruits and vegetables group.
He bought pork rinds
from the meat group.

And he bought fudge pops
from the chocolate group.

Dragon had a balanced diet.

He had so much food that he could not
fit it all into his car.
"I know what I will do," said Dragon.
"I will eat some of the food now,
and then the rest will fit in the car."

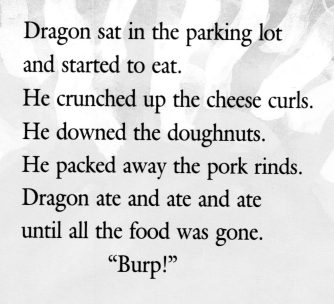

Dragon sat in the parking lot
and started to eat.
He crunched up the cheese curls.
He downed the doughnuts.
He packed away the pork rinds.
Dragon ate and ate and ate
until all the food was gone.
"Burp!"

Now *Dragon* could not fit into his car.
"Oh, what am I going to do?"
cried Dragon.
He thought and thought,
and scratched his big head.

"I know what I will do," said Dragon.
"I will push my car home."

So Dragon pushed his car down the hill.
The car began to roll faster
and faster . . .

and faster . . .

and faster.

Finally, Dragon's car came to a stop
right in front of his house.

All the excitement had made Dragon
very hungry.

He went into his kitchen
and looked in the cupboard.
There was no food at all.
"The cupboard is bare," said Dragon.
"Time to go shopping."

5
Good-night, Dragon

It had been a long, busy day,
and now it was bedtime.
Dragon was very groggy.
So he brushed his head
and combed his teeth. . . .

He watered his bed,
crawled into his plants . . .

. . . and fell fast asleep.

9